LAST RESORT

RICHARD WILLIAMS

Last Resort
Published in Great Britain in 2023
by Graffeg Limited.

Written by Richard Williams copyright © 2023.
Designed and produced by Graffeg Limited copyright
© 2023.

Graffeg Limited, 24 Stradey Park Business Centre,
Mwrwg Road, Llangennech, Llanelli,
Carmarthenshire, SA14 8YP, Wales, UK.
Tel: 01554 824000. www.graffeg.com.

The publisher acknowledges the financial support of
the Books Council of Wales. www.gwales.com.

Printed and bound in Great Britain by Clays Ltd,
Elcograf S.p.A.

ISBN 9781802584134

1 2 3 4 5 6 7 8 9

LAST RESORT

RICHARD WILLIAMS

For Nan

GRAFFEG

Part I

The Ebbing Tide

Prologue

February 1996

A man limps up the coast path at daybreak, back hunched, hands buried deep in his pockets. He stops to gaze down at the ocean below. His eyes widen and his shoulders fall limp.

At the mouth of the inlet lies an oil tanker, listing heavily to port. It is grounded on Box Reef, its colossal belly leaking oil into the pristine coastal waters of the Saltlands. The man watches as the blackness coils towards the nature reserve. The wind is calm, but the reek of oil fills his lungs.

A local fisherman from an ancient lineage, he has worked the Saltlands waters since he was a boy, when the misty mornings were the realm of mermaids and sea dragons. Now the dragon has finally arrived, casting darkness over the sea with its choking, swirling, oily rainbows.

The man takes out his tobacco tin. His trembling hands struggle to open it. He begins to roll a cigarette, glancing from the tin to the tanker and back down at his fingers, praying for it all to be a bad dream, but with each glance the morning lightens and the sea darkens.

He lights the cigarette and inhales.

A speedboat appears from behind the northern headland, cutting through the water towards the tanker. The fisherman narrows his eyes. He can see two men and a small boy aboard and a green flag flying proudly above it. The men are preparing to enter the maritime nightmare, but the little boy sits silently, looking backwards up at the cliffs where the fisherman is standing.

The fisherman looks down past his feet to the bottom of the cliff face. The noise of clean, crashing waves is replaced by gloopy slaps as the thick crude oil begins to smother the rocks. A tear rolls down his cheek and onto his lips. It stings like a welding spark and tastes of the sea.

He clasps his nape with his thick hand. His throat narrows and he begins to wheeze. He can hear his heart rate rising in his ears. The tanker starts to blur and the oil fumes feel overpowering.

He becomes disorientated, his heart thumps. He squints, trying to steady his feet. His mind scrambles for hope, but he knows that without his livelihood the landlord will evict them from the house in weeks. Only thoughts of his unborn child stop him from leaping off the edge of the world.

He hears a familiar noise nearby, like the rasping of a comb's teeth – the call of a razorbill. He peers further over the cliff edge, and there on a narrow ledge below is an all-black bird, one he doesn't recognise.

The bird cries again. It *is* a razorbill, but its noble white chest is gone. It's caked in oil. Its eyes are glued tight and its beak is pointed up in the air in confused submission. It calls again, but with less power. It attempts to raise its wings, but loses balance and falls sideways, its head crashing onto a rock.

The fisherman tosses his cigarette. Without a thought he lowers himself towards the bird, but his footing is treacherous on the slippery ledge. His right ankle twists and his knee buckles, pitching him forward. He throws out his arms to break his fall, but the camber of the damp grass rolls away from him. He bounces and slides, screaming off the edge of the cliff.

The boy on the boat gasps, closing his eyes before the fisherman hits the rocks. The boat races back towards the northern coastline and the boy remains silent, telling himself, over and over, it was just a bad dream.

Chapter 1

7 May 2021

'Have you been in a fight?' asks Ellie.

'No, Ma,' says Scott, sitting down heavily for breakfast. 'Just a late night.'

'Another one?'

'Yep. Got kicked out of the Three Crowns.'

'That's one of Cliffy John's, isn't it?'

'Aye. Banned from them all now.'

'Pathetic.'

Scott peers up through the sunlight, his eyes silvery and bloodshot. 'Don't start, Mother.'

She sighs.

The kitchen is warm and bright and smells of bacon and toast. All the appliances are old but well looked after. The sky-blue vinyl tablecloth is decorated with red roses and the old Portmeirion set still matches. Scott bends over and roughs up Mabel the dog's shag pile of hair.

Ellie sets the table around him. She's always on eggshells, but now it's gone too far. She's his mother.

She stands up straight, rests her palms on her narrow hips and says, 'Seriously, Scott, drinking yourself into oblivion day after day... Why? It's just not who you are.'

Puffing out his cheeks, Scott keeps his head down, stroking the dog. Calling him pathetic has rubbed him the wrong way. It clings.

'Answer me. It's every night, son. You had control of your life. You understood everything. You were always hunting for achievement and for things to look forward to. Don't go down this dead-end road now, *please*, Scott. You know how it ends.'

Scott sits up but avoids his mother's glare. He rolls his fingers on the edge of the wooden table and twitches his nose. He slides his chair backwards on the lino floor, crosses his arms, looks up and half-yells, 'Seriously. What the hell am I supposed to do? Tell me.'

Ellie drops her head.

'Tell me!'

'Calm down, Scott.' She scrambles for words, but none come.

'Everything's gotten worse, Ma, and none of it's my fault. Not a bit of it.'

'I know, son. I *know*. But it's just not you to throw in the towel like that. You've been a fighter since the day you were born.'

'This is different. And you know it.'

'I know. But this Covid has affected all of us. Not just you. Look around. We have to adapt. Think of how we can get through it. If all of the Saltlands just moped around getting pie-eyed on a Monday night the whole place would be a wasteland.'

'It already is.'

'No it's not, and you know it. We're lucky to be here. Imagine being stuck in a high-rise somewhere.'

'At least there'd be work there.'

Ellie sighs, removing her apron and placing it gently on the back of a chair. She turns to pick up the frying pan.

Scott feels a murmur in his gut. He's craving fat.

Ellie slides the two fried eggs and bacon onto his plate and sits down opposite him.

'Thanks,' he says, scraping butter onto his toast.

Scott takes a long swallow of orange juice and looks down at the glass.

Ellie frowns. 'You alright?'

'Sorry, my brain's just frazzled.'

'Nothing in the job centre then?'

'Nope.'

'Nothing at all?'

'Can't I just eat in peace here, Mother?'

'You know there's a lot more going on around here these days since the award – so many more tourists, and people moving down from away. That new Driftwood Café and the gastropub on Wibli Wobli Bay seem lovely. That's just the start, I'm sure.'

'Start of what?'

'Well... life! More people, Scott. Think about it – more people moving down with money, ideas, it's bound to lead to more businesses opening and work opportunities for the locals at some point.'

'They'll all disappear as soon as they've all had the vaccine and the virus is gone. This is just a mad blip. Nothing's gonna happen around here for a long time.'

'You don't think so?'

'Maybe in twenty years, when Pembrokeshire's finally gridlocked. Never forget that article, Ma. This is the Saltlands remember – the "Last Resort."'

'Well, times change, Scott.'

'Not round here. You know it's still a wasteland of rock and sand, and reeds and birds, and useless, uneducated, drunken sods like me.'

'Stop your nonsense.'

'It's true!'

'Well do something about it then.'

'I've tried. I'm thinking, but nothing's grabbed me yet.'

'What kind of thing are you thinking now?'

'Dunno.'

Silence.

'Maybe a bar, or coffee shop,' Scott says reluctantly.

'I see.'

'Not convinced, Ma?'

'Not really. I think you need to be outside. I dunno, maybe a tour guide or something? You'd be good at that. You're good with people.'

'Come on, Mother,' he says, mystified by her suggestion. 'Me? A tour guide? Chaperoning pensioners and English snobs around the coast path? Sod that for a game of soldiers. You're off your head.'

Scott takes a wild bite of his toast.

'Lifeguard?'

'Boring.'

'A job with the Parks?'

'Need a degree.'

'Fishing teacher?'

He looks up from his plate. 'Gimme a break, Mum, please.'

Silence returns.

Ellie swallows her next mouthful of food and puts down her knife. She inhales deeply and says, 'Are you sure you can't get the boat back?'

Scott stops chewing, puts down his cutlery. With one cheek still full of food he says, 'Absolutely sure,' with no hint of emotion, looking directly into his mother's eyes.

'Can you try? *Please*? It's blowing over, Scott. Business is bouncing back. The lorries are crossing the channel again now. And imagine all the crab out there after all these lockdowns,' she says with a strenuous, empty smile.

'Honestly, I can't believe I'm hearing this. You *knew* I had to sell the boat to keep this roof over our heads. Why on Earth do you keep banging on about it? We've been through this how many times?' he says, shaking his head.

'Can you please just try?'

'Why do you always do this?' he raises his voice and lurches across the table. 'Make me feel so guilty? You know I had no other option. Why, woman?'

'Stop it,' she says curtly. 'You should have discussed it with me first. It was my boat as well. We could have found a solution. You know it was your father's, and what he sacrificed to get it. It meant something, more than just fast cash to pay some bills.' Her voice breaks on the last words. Her hands tremor. She drops them under the table, out of sight.

He proceeds gently. 'Listen, Mum, you knew our debts – we couldn't sign up for more. We've been on the brink for years. And besides – and sorry to keep saying this – I wasn't even born when Dad died, so you can't keep putting that on me. It's not fair. How can I be so attached to his boat?'

Ellie could say a thousand words, but speaks none. 'You just don't understand.'

'Sorry, Mum, but it's *you* who doesn't understand.' He stands up. 'Dad took his own life. Remember that. He left us. So we have to just get on with it.'

She puts her hands over her face.

Seeing her helpless and brittle, he calms. He studies her for a while. Her hair is so thin he thinks about her skull beneath it. 'We have to move forward, Mum. Roll with the punches. It's 2021, not 1996. The world didn't end when we lost Dad. My life hadn't even started. You can't still be so sentimental about an old boat after twenty-odd years.'

She turns her head away from him.

He's static, blinking. Stalemate. Again. He turns, walks across the kitchen, picks up his wellies and exits through the back door.

Ellie wipes her eyes dry, stands up, slowly scrapes the half-eaten breakfast plates into a pile and carries the plate over to Mabel's bowl. She hunches down and runs her hands through the dog's waxy curls as it eats. Her hollow eyes stare into nothing.

Grinding his teeth, Scott climbs into the pick-up, ignites the heavy motor and speeds down the sand track towards the reserve. He can find no solace in his thoughts.

He stops at the shop for tobacco. When he walks in he feels different. He says 'Hi' to Clare on the till and he's sure she senses it too. There are two other customers, he's known them both all his life, but he suddenly feels unlike them. He thinks they are looking at him with hard eyes after they exchange hellos. Clare is especially nice to him at the checkout, magnifying his strangeness. He can't wait to get out.

A new weather system is approaching and Scott is driving towards it. The wind is whistling through the reedbeds as a hateful spew of black cloud stacks up all the way to the horizon like a giant tumour swirling towards the Saltlands coast.

The sky darkens. Everything around him begins to turn a different shade of blue. He slams the door of the pick-up, closes his jacket, tucks his chin under the sealed zipper and punches his hands deep into the pockets.

Underfoot the sand squeaks off his boots as he paces up over the dunes. The reedbeds sway and the talcum sand awakes, flitting around him with each new gust. He comes to a standstill at the top of the dune. Instead of assessing the sea as he does each daybreak, he closes his eyes. His nostrils flare as he inhales the thick, savoury smells of home until the new winds whip in a freshness from the ocean that blows the old scents away.

He lies down on his back in the cold sand, wiggling his body a comfy mould as the tide begins to fill the bay. He outstretches his arms and legs and gazes up at the fast moving clouds. The sea vapour moistens his face. He bites down hard on the inside of his cheek and whispers, 'Give me strength, Dad, please.' He has the coppery taste of blood in his mouth. 'Just give me some kind of sign that you didn't abandon me. Please.'

Chapter 2

Three days later, Scott goes overboard from the deck of a boat, tombstoning head first into the treacherous tidal waters of Mill Sound. He is swine-drunk. When he surfaces, Scott's world is serene and silent. He feels like he is floating in a liquid dream. He puts his head back and grins, sieving the salt water out of his teeth. With bloodshot eyes he looks up at the soft canopy of orange light.

It had been fourteen months since Scott's livelihood had been destroyed by one phone call, just two days after the start of the first Coronavirus pandemic lockdown in March 2020. Tulip Thomas, Scott's Chinese associate in Swansea, didn't mince her words when she informed him that his daily haul and supply of brown crab to China was to cease with immediate effect.

Scott was in the dockyard pressure-washing crab pots at the time. The first thing he remembered thinking was if Tulip was actually Tulip's real birth name. He concluded it couldn't have been, then reality hit Scott like a thunderbolt. He inhaled the old dockyard air and sensed its redundancy.

He hoofed the stack of crab pots and opened fire with the water gun, blasting the cages over the sea wall in his rage, through a haze of sopping mist and into the still dark waters of Saltlands dock.

The undertow of the fast-moving tidal waters swirls, sucking Scott under the surface. He knows he has to go with it. He holds his breath until he resurfaces, a mop of seaweed coiled around his head, twenty-five yards deeper inside the gurgling sound. He begins peeling it off, strand by strand.

The girl who is with him on the boat finally catches his eye. She's shouting to him, but nothing she yells reaches Scott's ears.

He submerges again, takes in some water, but feels no duty to save himself. He surfaces and observes the girl tossing a life buoy towards him. His mind is in a parallel space and he doesn't reach for it. He's detached from life and all its worries, and he experiences a moment of beautiful clarity.

It's only when the hard plastic buoy clobbers directly into his head that Scott shakes from his stupor. 'Hey!' he shouts up at the girl. 'That hit me on the head.' Scott grabs the bright red plastic ring. A minute later he's back in the boat. Three minutes later he's rolling a cigarette.

'I could have died then,' he says, philosophically, blowing out smoke.

'I know,' says the girl.

'No, I mean I *could* have died – could have *let myself* die, quite easily. It was a beautiful moment, until you slammed that buoy into my head.'

He can see she couldn't care less. He passes her the soggy roll-up.

'Saved your life,' she says, nonchalantly, plucking out the dangling wet tobacco shreds with her long nails before putting the butt into her mouth.

'You shouldn't have bothered.'

'Aye. I know.'

Scott smirks, shakes his head and looks out to sea.

The girl's name is Angie. She has just turned eighteen.

Angie came into Scott's life the previous night during a botched robbery. Her brother, Kippers, had stolen Scott's collection of vintage American fishing lures two years previously. The collection held strong sentimental value – it was started by

Scott's granddad on an exchange to Wisconsin in 1974, and carried on by his father through the eighties and nineties, until his suicide in 1996. The antiquated oak box housed a Heddon Night Radiant lure, a Comstock Flying Hellgrammite, and a replica of the rare Heddon Frog, dating back to the early fifties. The collection was estimated to be worth over ten thousand pounds – no mean sum for a fisherman teetering on the brink of bankruptcy.

Kippers had stolen the treasure from the back of Scott's van during the 2019 Saltlands Fish Week. Scott had brought them out to display during the traditional maritime celebration. They drew large crowds of interested observers – not least of all Kippers.

Kippers, a dockyard cleaner, had been overheard bragging of his theft to Donna, the barmaid of the dockyard pub, The Mighty Oak, while draining pints of cider on the eve of the first lockdown. Now, sixteen months later, Scott wanted them back, no, *needed* them back, to pay bills and stay afloat.

Since Kippers still denied ever taking them, Scott knew he had to go to Kipper's house in Atlantic Drive to recoup them himself.

Atlantic Drive was the heart of the docklands community – a microcosm of domestic violence, inter-family feuds, DIY car repairs, drug peddling, prolific procreation and second-hand sunbed trading. Tanning was serious business in the Saltlands, and Atlantic Drive had the highest density of home solariums in the west. Shards of UV light burst out from most dwellings in the depths of winter and the streetlights famously flickered until well past midnight.

From a distance, Atlantic Drive's ladies resembled Scandinavian goddesses. From close up, not so much. The street had a 'posh end', and Kippers lived at the other end with his parents and sister, Angie.

Kipper's dad, Gary, was notorious in the Saltlands. This was no mean feat given the dockland's long heritage of seafaring thugs. At eighteen he became infamous for beating up a policeman and peeing on his shoes, but he gained greater notoriety years later for having dug out a fish pond in his lounge floor where he kept six dwarf Koi carp, and for housing a live donkey, Bert, in the spare bedroom. Neutralising Bert was key to pulling off the robbery, so Scott filled his pockets with a wad of sliced carrots and pears.

Scott had calculated the best time to strike this family of helpless drunks.

During the daytime would be impossible –

Gary and Eula had been on the sick for years. Housebound. Most days, Gary fried sausages and ranted at the kitchen telly, while Eula sang online karaoke with her family back in the Philippines.

Scott entered the house at 4.30am on a Sunday. He didn't technically break in – the back door was wide open.

The smell of stale cigarettes and alcohol washed over him and he immediately felt nauseous. Moments later, gazing into the homemade fishpond he was bamboozled by the sight of slithering dwarf Koi carp embedded into the carpet of the council house floor.

With carrots and pears gripped in both hands, Scott turned and stepped towards Kipper's bedroom. But there was no sight or sound of Bert.

By focusing on the donkey, Scott had overlooked one very important aspect of the break-in – Angie. She stepped out from the darkness the moment Scott arrived at her brother's bedroom door.

He froze and his eyes latched onto Angie's.

'I know you,' said Angie, quietly, without a hint of nerves. 'What are you doing in my house?'

Scott stuttered, 'Erm... I... I've come for my fishing lures. Your brother nicked them off me during Fish Week a couple of years ago. I need them back to pay some bills, otherwise me and my mother are gonna get kicked out of our house.'

'I know he took them.'

'Really?' Scott said, surprised. 'So you know where they are?'

'Yep.'

'Can you get them for me?'

'Nope.'

'Why not?'

'Well, I can. On one condition.'

'What's that?'

Angie paused. She eased herself forward, still holding Scott's gaze. 'You take me with you.'

'What do you mean? Where?'

'I don't care. Just out of here.'

'I can't do that!'

'Why not?'

'Because!'

'I'll get your box of hooks, and we go, right now, together. And I stay with you for a bit, until I sort myself out. That's the deal. Or else I'll scream.'

'They're lures, not hooks.'

'Whatever... it's Scott, isn't it? Make your mind up, and quick, Scotty boy.'

Scott felt sick at the idea of taking her home. He scanned the ramshackle room for an answer. What was he going to do with her? She was bonkers, just like her father. If he wasn't drowned now he was just postponing death if he kidnapped Gary Pritchard's little girl.

Scott took a deep breath and said, 'Just get the lures and let's get out of here.'

Two nosey seagulls fly low over the boat. One squawks. Scott notices a small smile break on Angie's face for the first time.

He admires her as she smokes, staring out to sea, lost in her thoughts. Her brown Eurasian skin softens her high, chiselled cheekbones and her dark chestnut hair dances around her head like wildfire. She turns to him and takes another deep drag. Scrunching her face against the rising smoke she says, 'What's occurring then, you muppet?'

His eyes ping skywards. 'Can't you just enjoy the moment, Angie? And stop looking for a fight every minute you're bored, please.' He shakes his head and relaxes back onto the hard wooden bench seat.

Angie is not amused.

He raises his hands into the air and swishes them around slowly, still half-drunk. 'Look where we are! Look at that sky. Does it get any more beautiful?'

Angie remains silent, taking in the vista of

ancient sea cliffs, the open ocean and the distant islands silhouetted under the dark orange sky. She nods approvingly, turns to Scott and says, 'Did you just try to kill yourself back there?'

His body goes taut, his smile fades. He props himself up on his elbows, the ends of his dreadlocks rest on the deck. The deep furrows of his sun-ravaged forehead frown up at Angie until a defiant grin appears on his face. He starts to giggle, and giggle, and soon to laugh out loud, crossing his arms across his stomach, rolling sideways.

It's infectious. Angie begins to chuckle, then to laugh. In thirty seconds the pair are howling like hyenas on the small boat, alone on the big open sea, the thick seams of black sky consuming the last of the tangerine ribbons draped over the distant horizon.

A cool wind passes over and they fall silent. Just the sound of soft slapping waves bounce against the hull.

Angie reaches for her sweater. She pulls it over her head. Before threading her arms, she says, 'Where are we headed now then? Back to the dockyard? Or the Bahamas? Barbados? I'm game.'

Scott looks over the endless Atlantic to the south-west, knowing that the Caribbean was merely a straight line away through this very ocean. If it wasn't for her father he'd be willing to chance it. She's the most beautiful girl he's ever seen. He's enjoying her company, but she's nuts, and her father's psychotic. He chooses the long game – safety first, he doesn't need any more trouble. 'Just the glorious Saltlands dockyard, I'm afraid, love, gotta give the boat back,' he says, without making eye contact.

She smirks, a little put out, not used to a brush-off. She slips into the sweater, suppressing the fizz of lust that's bubbling inside her.

Scott steps up to the helm and fires up the engine. The boat cuts through the blackening sea towards the mouth of the inlet.

Chapter 3

Later that evening, two men arrive like spectres through the heavy fog of sea mist, their boat slicing through the jet-black ocean towards the Saltlands dockyard. They shuffle down the deck towards the bow, one large and lurching, the other shorter and nimble. They both inspect their tackle bags before heaving them over the gunwale, stepping off the boat and onto the dimly lit jetty.

Midnight. They enter through the kitchen door of The Greyhound. Dai winces at the stench of bleach and stale beer. He says, 'Jesus, Cliffy, sort this ventilation out, boyo.'

Cliffy frowns, shakes his head and pads the tiled wall, feeling for the light switch. They waddle through the tiny kitchen with their tackle bags swinging like pendulums between their legs and into the Back Bar, where they drop them onto the dusty floor. Not more than a minute later, they open them up and begin counting thick wads of twenty-pound notes.

The Greyhound was Councillor Cliffy John's first pub purchase back in 2008 after selling his successful second-hand car business. The pub comprises two simple boxed rooms with bench seating. One large room – the generously named 'Lounge' – and one small – the 'Back Bar' – designed and constructed away from the windows, most likely for the purpose of lock-ins.

Just beer, spirits and crisps at The Greyhound, no food (the kitchen is too small). Despite having only three regular alcoholics, Cliffy retains a soft spot for this lifeless establishment but has never spent a penny to improve it.

The Back Bar is the counting house. It feels safe – dark, with just a soft orange glow from the glass coals of the electric fire, creating a private, intimate space. The bleak walls are covered in garishly framed illustrations of greyhound meets and fox hunts, the types you find in charity shops for a pound, and there is a single ale pump behind the make-do bar for Cliffy's favourite beer – Felinfoel Double Dragon.

'It's getting tricky now, Dai,' says Cliffy, still thumbing the notes intently.

'What's that?' asks Dai.

'Running all this cash through these empty tills.'

'Aye, you said that before.'

'No, now I mean it's pretty much impossible.'

Dai stops counting, looks up. 'Why's that?'

'Well, turnover's dwindling to almost zero.'

Dai frowns, looks surprised. 'Don't be daft, you must have plenty of cash coming in with all the drinkers round here?'

'They're all drinking at home now since the lockdowns. Got used to it. Special Brew, fags and Sky TV in the comfort of their own homes. And all the kids are going to that new gastropub on Wibli Wobli Bay, drinking all that craft beer piss. I'm lucky if I get a couple hundred quid a week some weeks, it's so dead. We can't keep running cash through the tills at the rate we've been doing.'

'Why don't you sell craft beer as well then?'

'Sod that, Dai. Real drinkers don't drink craft beer. Too much hops and that. You can't fire pints of it down your neck. It's like treacle. Those kids will spend all night nursing a pint, convincing themselves it's the best thing since chocolate.'

'There we are then,' says Dai, smirking, but the worried look on Cliffy's face unnerves him. 'Something happened?'

'Dunno. Maybe,' says Cliffy, rolling his fingernails over a small patch of dry skin on his protruding jawline. 'There's just been a few odd clients lately. Misfits – blokes I'm sure would never normally be coming in.'

'Tax office?'

'Possibly. Or the bank. They're all tightening up.'

Cliffy stands up, walks over to the bar, takes two glasses and pumps them full of Double Dragon. Off-white soapy bubbles spill out over the first glass and slide down the tankard.

Dai sighs. He puts the pile of notes down on the carpet next to his knee. 'Christ, I dunno. Maybe we should knock the whole lot on the head, Cliff.'

Cliffy looks up, startled, still dragging the base of the glasses along the towelled beer mat. 'Why?' he snipes. 'Don't tell me Inspector "Big" Dai Harries is getting the heebie-jeebies? Or worse, a guilty conscience.' A former county scrum-half, at five foot three Dai stands a full inch taller than both his siblings.

Dai pulls a face while Cliffy sucks the head off one of the pints. He licks the foam off his lips with a neat swipe of his tongue. His glass glints in the electric firelight. He hands the other pint to Dai.

'Huh. I'm a bent copper, Cliff. My conscience died a long time ago.'

'Good job too. Here.' Cliffy throws Dai a packet of pork scratchings.

Dai catches it and puts it down next to the pile of notes. 'But it's not just the money, Cliff. It's this Black Tar as well,' Dai says, tailing to a whisper. 'That's the stuff that's killing all those kids. We have to draw a line. We shouldn't be privy to this stuff coming in through our shores.'

Cliffy bolts upright, rests his bloated belly on the bar and folds his arms with self-righteous confidence. 'Look, Dai – let me reiterate, all we do is turn a blind eye to stuff that's coming in through the coast. Sod all else. You know that. We're not heroin dealers. If those smack heads want a fix, they're gonna get it from somewhere, whether it comes through Conor or not. My conscience is clean. Yours should be too. It's bugger all to do with us.'

Dai studies his old friend for a moment. Cliffy's bloated face looks malignant in the crimson glow of the fire. Dai knows that behind the affable local councillor smile is the attitude of a thug. Dai doesn't reply, he drops his head and picks out another wad from the bag.

'We can't stop now, Dai,' Cliffy says firmly. 'We're up to our nuts in it. Let's just keep going a bit longer, set ourselves up a bit more. We'll have to give Conor a few months notice anyway. We can't just drop him like that. He'll have us cut up.'

'Aye. I know.'

'But like I said, it'll all have to slow down now anyway, Dai, even scale down a bit for it to be sustainable. We can't have all this cash just lying around. I'll ask Conor if he can cut back a bit.'

'Ha!' Dai looks up. A forlorn grin strains his face. 'Cut back? Conor? You're not right in the head, Cliff. He's on a roll, and getting more nuts and reckless as time ticks on.'

'What do you mean?'

'More wealthy, more powerful, more isolated, more paranoid.'

'Aye, you're right,' says Cliffy, suddenly pondering. 'I find him very temperamental these days. Very difficult to have a conversation with. He's not the nice lad he used to be, is he?'

Dai sniggers nasally, shakes his head. Cliffy takes a deep breath and drains his pint.

'And the cash is gonna keep coming too, Cliff. No fear of that.'

Cliffy goes long-faced, twitches his nose.

They stop talking and turn their gaze to the fire.

'Careful what you wish for, Cliff,' Dai says quietly, wiping the clamminess off his cheeks.

With his eyes still entranced by the twirling electric fire, Cliffy rubs his face with both hands. He stands up and looks down at the wads of cash strewn on the sticky paisley carpet. 'We'll be fine,' he asserts, rubbing his face again.

Dai's not convinced. He knows only an idiot wouldn't be scared out of their mind.

Chapter 4

The following evening, Scott takes Angie out for dinner and drinks at the newly opened Kung Fu Diner in Holetown.

The large, empty restaurant is a confused hash of black wood panelling, red velvet curtains and cheaply framed calligraphic dragons and ancient warriors of the East.

Scattered amongst these on the old dancefloor are four real cars – three Dacia Logans and a Nissan Micra. On the stage stand life-size cutouts of John Wayne and Bruce Lee. Together, they qualify the establishment as a legitimate 'diner', at least to the restaurant's new owner, Tom Parry.

Tom had bought the Chinese restaurant in February, a month before the first lockdown. He was known for his bad luck. His ambitious plans to convert the historic county bingo hall turned car garage turned Chinese dining emporium into a warehouse-style rustic-industrial diner were scuppered by the impact of Covid-19. With the lockdown came no cash flow and an unending stream of hidden costs. Tom's renovation budget was swallowed up within weeks, leaving him with just £789 to convert the Chinese into the glitzy Warehouse Diner. All Tom could afford was the four cars from the scrap yard and the cut outs from the Internet. The dismal Chinese décor remained, and the Kung Fu Diner was born.

Scott and Angie are sitting in the front seats of a green Dacia Logan on the dancefloor of the Diner.

Tom arrives to take their order.

Scott smiles, eases back in his seat. 'Bloody hell... Tommy Parry.' Scott remembers brawling regularly with Tom on the rugby pitch, years ago. Scott played for Docklands Juniors, Tom for Holetown.

Tom steps back, genuinely surprised. 'Scott Ellis... sorry, didn't recognise you with those dreads, man. Been ages. How are you keeping?'

'You don't wanna know, Tom.'

'I can guess, mate, don't worry. Same here. Look at me,' Tom says, brushing his hands from his head to his hips, cringing.

Tom is wearing a white kimono and a Japanese flag bandana.

'What the hell is this place?' says Scott, almost struggling to breathe through laughter.

'It's all the renovation work I could afford!' says Tom, equally amused. 'I had big plans for a contemporary diner, all rustic and industrial, but I couldn't afford to fully renovate once Covid hit. So I improvised.'

'I think it's cool,' says Angie. 'Bonkers, but cool.'

Tom's expression soon changes. 'Well, it's not really cool. I'm losing money every day, to be honest. Money that's not mine.'

Clocking some newly arriving guests, Tom says, 'What can I get you, mate? We'll have a chat later, gotta dash. I'm on my own here tonight, can't afford staff at the mo.'

Scott nods knowingly and orders two pints of lager and two Jägerbombs.

With the second round, less than ten minutes later, they order two burgers.

As the alcohol takes effect, Scott and Angie go beyond the motiveless chitchat.

'So why did you sell your boat?' asks Angie, her eyes wide and glazed.

'Don't *you* start,' he says, fiddling with the indicator stick.

'Seems fishing is picking up again now,' she says, her voice almost dancing. 'Kippers is flat out down the dockyard. Trucks are running to the continent again and there's talk of crab going back to China again soon.'

Scott shakes his head. 'That ain't gonna happen.'

'Why not?'

'Just isn't. Waste of time. First Covid, now the Brexit deal. Fishing is doomed.'

'Jesus, you're good company,' she says, before knocking her drink back, keeping the pace.

'Piss off. You got onto the subject,' he says, half-serious. 'Anyway, only the big boats stand a chance these days. It's like anything. It's like an arms race round here for crabs. Some boats have got thousands of pots now. I only had eighty when I sold up. Glad to see the back of it all. It's not the same anymore, you must see that?'

'Suppose.'

Angie goes quiet, looks at him oddly.

He notices. 'What's up?'

'Can I ask you a personal question?'

'Er, yeah, course.'

She pauses for a moment then says, 'Wasn't it your dad who killed himself on the day of that big oil spill?'

Scott's head rears back. He studies her face, knowing she was born years after the event. 'Er, yeah, that's the official verdict, but most people say he would never have done it. They reckon it was an accident. He slipped.' He tilts his head, frowns. 'Why do you ask anyway? Who told you about that?'

Angie feels awkward, kicks herself for bringing it up. 'Well, I think everyone round here knows about it. It sounds like it was a pretty big deal at the time.'

Scott turns and stares out of the windscreen. He begins to gnaw on his thumbnail. 'But still, sometimes I doubt people. I think they're just trying to protect me, and I wonder if he did actually jump. I was only born eight weeks later, you know.' He looks across at Angie. 'Why would any man want to kill himself knowing he had a son on the way?'

She looks into his blue-grey eyes and feels his suffering. 'Trust those who knew him best,' she says tenderly.

Her words surprise and affect him. 'I try to. But it's not that easy.'

They fall silent.

Scott looks down into his lap.

Angie looks out through the windscreen. She sees Tom running around with plates and feels pity for him and his forced enthusiasm towards the other diners. He looks so lonely to her.

'Anyway,' says Scott, lifting his head, 'you know how it used to be round here, Angie. The dockyard was rockin'. And look at it now, a wasteland.'

She spins to face him, looking baffled. 'What? No, it's not. The place is heaving! When was the last time you went to Wibli Wobli Bay? Never been so many new people and tourists around here.'

'I meant for fishing.'

'Well do something else then.'

'Jesus,' Scott squeezes his eyes and rattles his head. 'Let's stop talking about me. What about *you*? What are you doing with your life?'

Just as Angie is about to speak, four young men brush past their table as they enter the diner, all in bright polo shirts, two with sunglasses still sitting on the top of their heads.

The men, clearly not locals, approach Tom at the bar and ask loudly for the nearest casino.

Tom laughs. Scott too. Their eyes meet.

Tom explains the nearest casino is probably in Cardiff, a hundred miles away. The four men's eyes close slowly in unison, like dying swans. They turn and walk out of the door.

Scott's imagination tingles. Mystical notions spin in his head. He goes dead quiet. He notices Tom glancing back over at him.

'Cat got your tongue?' says Angie, before licking the salt off the stem of her thumb and throwing the Tequila down her throat.

'Of course,' he yelps, fevered with excitement, 'a casino, a Saltlands casino!'

'You serious?' Angie's eyelashes flutter as she bites down and sucks on the slice of lemon.

Scott's eyes widen. 'That's it!' He points madly at Angie's eyes, 'The Flutter Club!'

'What?'

'Just then, your eyes, they fluttered!' He grabs her by the shoulders. 'To bet is to flutter,' he says, eyes sparkling. 'Get it?'

'Er, suppose so.' Angie's mind swims up slowly through the alcohol, trying to join the dots.

'All this time wasted thinking about all the rubbish jobs I could do around here!'

'OK, OK, calm down, man,' she says, patting her hands in the air between them. 'Same again?' she asks.

'Aye,' he says, his mind adrift.

By 11pm Scott and Angie are the only ones left in the diner.

Tom approaches with a beer and asks if he can join them.

'Sure thing, Tommy,' says Scott. 'Hop in the back of the wagon.'

Tom climbs into the back seat of the car and sits down. 'So how was everyth—'

'CASINO!' yells Scott, swivelling his body towards Tom.

Angie closes her eyes with embarrassment.

Tom bursts out laughing. 'You think?'

'I think. *You* think,' says Scott, jabbing a drunken finger into Tom's bare chest. 'Don't deny it, Tommy boy. We had a moment back there.'

Tom nods. 'We did.'

'So what do you reckon?'

'Well, I'd definitely think about it. This place is a waste of time.'

Scott asks, 'How much do you reckon we'd need to invest to turn this place into a basic casino, Tom?'

'No idea. But if we shopped around it wouldn't cost too much. I often see blackjack and roulette tables on eBay and industry websites. Structurally we have everything – the bar, kitchen, good ventilation. Those are the main things. Honestly, it's mostly just décor and furniture.'

'And the licence,' says Scott. 'Getting that can't be easy.'

'Yeah...' Tom says in a slow drawl. 'I'll need to look into that.'

Angie steps out of the car, folds her arms and looks around. 'It has to look nice,' she says intently, 'and be warm and inviting. It's a big space. It'll cost a fair whack I bet.'

Scott and Tom clamber out of the car.

Tom stands next to Angie.

Scott grips the open door and rests his chin on its frame. He quietly rocks back and forth while he thinks.

The three of them scan the big room. It looks more landscaped than furnished. The hard rain draws their attention up to the domed glass roof section above them.

'It's all here,' says Scott. 'It's a beautiful building.'

'Aye,' says Tom, nodding. 'That's why I jumped on the chance. Just my concept is rubbish.'

'Well, Tommy,' says Scott, standing up straight. 'I've still got a few grand stashed away after selling the boat, and I can probably get another decent chunk if I can sell my vintage collection of fishing lures. So I reckon I could put at least fifteen grand in, if you're looking for a partner.'

Tom looks at Scott for a long moment. The rain lashes harder on the glass dome. Tom says, 'Yeah, but going into business with people is a big risk, Scott. I've seen it in my family. As soon as money comes into play, relationships can go tits up, pretty damn quick. And we don't know if we could even work together, do we? Christ, I haven't seen you for years.'

'Come on, man,' says Scott, rankled. 'We used to knock seven bells out of each other on the rugby pitch, for how long?'

'*Ooof*, dunno. Probably six or seven years.'

'Exactly. Teamwork, grit, determination, it's what we've grown up with, Tom. It's what we're made of. We have that history together, man. You know I've been fishing flat out all my life until recently. All I've ever known is hard work.'

'Yeah, I know, mate,' Tom says without hesitation. Then he pauses. 'You're seriously up for it? A *casino*?'

'Mate, I'm *mad* for it.'

'Me too,' says Angie. 'I don't have any cash, but I'll earn my keep. I'm sure I can help.'

'Really?' says Tom, looking at Angie, then Scott.

'Look, Tommy. We're not the most stable human beings in the world, if we're honest, are we, Angie?'

Angie shakes her head and shrugs.

'But we're so full of energy. And a casino in the Saltlands right now would clean up. The place is bouncing with cash with all the new imports and tourists. And there's hardly anything around here to spend it on. People must be loaded, being locked down and not spending for the best part of what, eighteen months?'

Tom nods, and asks, 'What would we call it?'

Scott glances at Angie, then turns to Tom.

'How about The Flutter Club?'

Tom remains still. His eyes slide away from Scott and roll around the venue like a curious chameleon's, conceptualising the proposition. Slowly, he begins to nod. 'The Flutter Club,' he says. 'The Saltlands' first ever casino...' He turns back to Scott and extends his hand towards him through his gaping kimono sleeve and says, 'I got nothing to lose. Let's do it, bro.'

On the walk back home, Scott's excitement begins to irritate Angie; she can't get a word in edgeways. And she's craving him. As they approach the end of Atlantic Drive she slaps her hand onto Scott's chest, stopping him in his tracks. She pushes him forcefully backwards into a lamppost, its fuzzy orange glow drenching their faces. Scott smiles. Angie tilts her head and presses her lips against his.

Chapter 5

The application for a casino licence lands at the Saltlands council offices like a bomb. With a lump of Scott's investment, Tom has recruited a consultant to assist with the entire application process to the Gambling Commission. The application is, by some measure, bulletproof, set to attract people and other businesses and creating more jobs and tax revenue.

Word from the Commission hints that the application meets all requirements for a small casino operating licence. There is just the not-so-small matter of attaining a casino premises licence from the notoriously conservative Saltlands District Council, which will have to authorise a change in activity at the Kung Fu Diner premises from a restaurant into a fully fledged casino.

Councillor Cliffy John is informed of the Flutter Club application by chance. Fellow councillor Terry Watkins appears next to him outside the

Contented Sole chip shop in Holetown and blurts out the exciting news just as Cliffy is fingering the tail end of an entire battered sausage into his mouth. As the sausage disappears, Cliffy almost chokes.

He is soon on the phone to Dai. They agree unanimously – only over their dead bodies would this licence be approved.

Cliffy cancels his one-to-one salsa class at the community centre, drives straight home and hoofs the cat against the Aga.

During the first twenty-seven days of the public notice period of the application there are no representations made against the proposed Flutter Club. The fact that many locals are established gambling addicts and alcoholics likely helps. But on the last day – day twenty-eight – three objections arrive at the council offices. One from Baptist minister Islwyn Rees, one from Councillor Cliffy John and one decisive objection from the Saltlands' police force, signed by Inspector Dai Harries.

Rev. Rees cites concerns of gambling and drinking on the more vulnerable sections of society, as well as the principal hours of business being late night – not compatible with the Saltlands way of life. The casino's activities will likely result in increased public nuisance.

Cliffy John's objection cites the likelihood of the casino becoming a 'den of iniquity' characterised by consistent anti-social behaviour. This raises a few eyebrows within the council ranks.

Dai Harries's letter on behalf of the police force expresses grave concern that the Saltlands' crime and disorder objective will be undermined by the likely impact of casino activities, which is difficult for the licensing officers to disagree with.

All three objections are weighted and compelling, yet opinions at the district council remain divided.

The Flutter Club business plan is professional and convincing, with a five-year budget and workplan and a compliance framework that impresses even the Gambling Commission. But more than that, many tacit community leaders look upon Tom and Scott as hard-working young men of the community that can help carry the Saltlands into the future.

The licensing team arrange a hearing in front of a Licensing Sub-Committee to determine the outcome of the application. Tom and Scott are invited, and the whole of the Saltlands holds its breath.

The Sub-Committee meeting in Holetown

church hall does not start well for Tom and Scott. After Rev Rees says his piece in a measured and sincere manner, Cliffy jumps in and makes a full-on assault on the immorality of the Flutter Club plans.

Given Cliffy's history as publican to the most notorious pubs in the Saltlands, his motives and intentions are questionable to the Sub Committee members. There is a clear conflict of interest. However, Inspector Dai Harries's unwavering support for Cliffy is compelling.

But Tom and Scott are honest and humble and they defend themselves and their project well. They are local boys from local working families going back generations, and it is widely known that the pair have endured more than their fair share of adversity over the years.

Both give personal assurances to the Sub-Committee that the Flutter Club would be run tidily, respectfully and in keeping with the Saltlands' community spirit. They propose sensible opening times for the first twelve months – closing at 10pm, no later, even on weekends, with music limits set to 85db, a noise level that would not be heard outside the premises.

The Sub-Committee confers.

Cliffy eyeballs Scott. He can't stand the lad. He's glad he's managed to ban him from all his pubs, cocky little bastard.

Scott blows him a kiss.

Blood shoots into Cliffy's face.

The Sub-Committee announces that the premises licence for the Flutter Club is approved, with a number of strict conditions.

Dai and Cliffy are stunned.

Tom and Scott embrace.

With his arms still wrapped around Tom's back, Scott flicks Cliffy the middle finger.

Cliffy glares back. He grinds down on his teeth and his jowls ripple. This is clearly not the end of the matter.

News of the Flutter Club's approval spreads like bushfire through the Saltlands, and within twenty-four hours excitement levels reach fever pitch.

PART II

The Gathering Storm

Chapter 6

Six weeks after the approval of the Flutter Club, an English orthodontist named Jim Peasnell is alone, drinking a latte. He's sitting on the terrace of the newly opened Driftwood Eco Café on a sand dune overlooking Wibli Wobli Bay, the crown jewel of the Saltlands National Park. Jim has been holidaying in this part of west Wales for decades. He's enamoured with a sense of pride at how the bay has developed from an armpit of desolation into one of the UK's top beach holiday destinations. Despite the cranes, building sites, new cafés and shops splattered along the coastline, the development is, by and large, in keeping with the environment – the housing is all wooden, built to high ecological specifications, and all single story, set in trees.

Jim is equally proud of the price he paid for his caravan twenty-four years previously, just weeks after *that* travel review in the *Sunday Times*, back in the days when the bay was called Oldwinds.

Oldwinds was renamed Wibli Wobli Bay in

2004, after thousands of Portuguese Man-O-War jellyfish washed up on its golden sands, closing the bay for an entire summer season, decimating local tourism. But crisis was flipped to opportunity by Jude, a bright young marketing assistant from the Saltlands tourism office who came up with the name Wibli Wobli, the Welsh colloquial name for jellyfish, and the council loved it.

Within weeks of the formal renaming, Jude was catapulted to the red sofa of *BBC Breakfast* to convey the story that had already begun to capture the nation's imagination in both the tabloids and broadsheets. Images of the pristine and desolate horseshoe bay in one of Wales's most remote corners filled TV screens all over Britain, and from that moment on, Wibli Wobli Bay was a national beach destination, and its days of desolation were numbered.

Jim's latte tastes exquisite compared to the coffee he used to drink when the place was the old Red Lobster Café. He always imagined that stuff had been percolated through a fisherman's dirty sock.

He begins to eavesdrop on the neighbouring table. At the same time he's admiring the latte art inside his mug. The patterned foam is stubbornly resisting his short, high-suction sips as he drains the coffee from under it.

Next to him are two old men. Locals. Jim suspects fishermen by the way they dress and swear, or maybe farmers. They're discussing the latest Saltlands accolade, and tempers are unravelling.

A storm cloud approaches and the old boys carry their argument inside. The remaining clients follow, shuffling into the glassed room. But not Jim. He's going for a swim. He walks onto the sand with his towel under his arm and up the beach into a dense squall of warm rain. He has never felt so happy and free.

Jim is a good orthodontist, but not such a good swimmer. He fails to return to the holiday park for supper. His wife, Denise, calls the police at 10pm.

During a torch-lit search, Jim's clothes are found on the sand. The policemen do not say, but Denise can see in their eyes that her husband is presumed dead. She regrets the fact that her last conversation with Jim was not a loving one and laments admitting this to the police.

The lifeboat is called. It launches into the dark, turbulent ocean twenty minutes later, returning forty minutes after that. No Jim.

The search will resume at first light.

Due to the afternoon rain storm the beach

had emptied. No witnesses.

The bay is notorious for its rip currents, but Denise knows Jim is careful in the water. He'd been swimming in the bay for years.

Denise is visited on the night of Jim's disappearance by local police Inspector Dai Harries. Denise pours out two cups of tea and Dai sits down.

His questioning begins.

Big Dai's line of inquiry unsettles Denise. In fact, she is stunned. She feels more of a suspect than a victim. Her teacup rattles like a distant alarm bell on the porcelain saucer sitting in the palm of her hand.

Dai notices. He whips a pen out from his shirt pocket, uncaps it with his teeth and writes down just three words.

Denise places her tea calmly down on the tablecloth as Dai shields his notepad with a cupped hand.

Dai leaves ten minutes later.

Denise prays to God for Jim to walk back through the door. She is sure he is still alive.

The search resumes at 7.15am – the lifeboat out to sea, police and lifeguards on foot around the rocky coastline.

There is no sign of Jim. The search is called off by nightfall.

Jim Peasnell is missing, presumed dead.

Denise makes enquiries about Jim's belongings. Along with his clothes, his glasses, a towel and his prescription swimming goggles were found. Immediately, she knows he did not enter the water. At least not voluntarily.

She tells Inspector Harries that things don't add up. He frowns, a look of inconvenience more than enquiry. He says he'll look into it. He makes his excuses and leaves.

Chapter 7

The next morning, Jim Peasnell is woken by the chattering of his own teeth. The left side of his neck aches. He finds himself looking up at the jagged ceiling of a cave. He tries to right himself and feels the harsh rub of rope against his wrists.

He looks across to where three young men are huddled around the dying embers of a campfire. One is twiddling a stick into the ash. All three look like they are lost in their own silent daydreams.

The trio all have long, shaggy hair – two brunettes, one blond, all wearing thick, woolly cardigans with patterned designs that could have come from anywhere between India and Peru.

They have not noticed that Jim is awake.

Jim rolls himself up onto his knees and says, 'Hello?' in a crusty warble.

Both brunette boys turn towards him, startled, as Jim's voice echoes around the deep cave.

'Good morning, old boy,' says the blond one, whose gaze hasn't moved from the fire.

'Who are you?' asks Jim.

The blond one lifts his head, looks across at Jim and says proudly, 'We are the Sons of Blodwyn.'

Jim frowns. 'What? What does that mean? Who's Blodwyn?'

'The heroine of the last invasion of Britain, you fool. She fought off the French invaders and saved these lands from foreign scum like you.'

Jim looks puzzled. He racks his brain. He's sure that's not right.

'We're the protectors of the Saltlands. Protectors from you English vermin and every other mindless tourist who comes to destroy our land.'

Jim can't believe his ears. 'What do you mean? *You're* English.'

'No, I'm not,' the blond boy scowls. 'I was born here,' he says in perfect King's English.

'Doesn't sound like it,' Jim says mockingly, his inhibitions still dampened by the drugs.

The blond boy leaps up, slings the stick and paces purposefully across the cave. The shingle crunches under his haggard espadrilles and his orange Thai fisherman pants flap around his white needle-thin shins.

As the boy bounds towards him, Jim's heartbeat whips up and begins to throb in his throat.

A smirk appears on the boy's face.

Jim clenches.

A single blow hammers across Jim's cheek. The sound resonates. He yelps and falls like a skittle, his head crashing onto the damp shingle.

The two brunette boys make O shapes with their mouths and look at each other, saying nothing.

'Horacio Fox!' screams the blond boy down at Jim Peasnell. 'Remember that name, you English pig.'

Blood trickles from the corner of Jim's mouth. He whimpers.

Horacio Fox was born and raised in the remote hills of northern Saltlands, but his upbringing was far from conventional. His parents were reclusive and unhinged environmentalists who sought the good life of isolated self-sufficiency on their lonely rural outpost.

Horacio's father, Barnaby – youngest son of Lord Fox of Virginia Water, Surrey – had dropped out of Cambridge to join Greenpeace in 1988. While on an investigative mission into illegal logging in the Peruvian Amazon, Barnaby succumbed to the temptation of *ayahuasca*, a psychedelic brewed by local shamen. Without warning, he abandoned his mission and disappeared into the jungle, following a four-foot shaman wearing Nike Air Jordans and a Rolex. He reappeared some three months later, naked and lacerated, just a snakeskin fez encrusted onto his head.

After hitching to Lima, Barnaby called his brother, Sam, to help him purchase a plane ticket back to London. During the conversation, Barnaby announced that he was now both a psychedelic preacher *and* an MI6 agent, having been recruited by the spy agency while on his foray into the jungle.

Sam prepared the family for the worst.

On his return to Virginia Water, Barnaby constructed a rickety soapbox to preach sacred geometry from outside the local Tesco, and to monitor for any potential terrorist activity. On the same day, he was ostracised from the family and his trust fund was frozen.

A relocation into obscurity was inevitable. Barnaby followed the trail of the Stonehenge bluestones all the way to their source in west Wales. He eventually bought a derelict smallholding nearby in the hills of northern Saltlands with a last payout from his father.

Six months later, at a protest outside a Pembrokeshire oil refinery, he met Stella, an environmentalist with a range of personality disorders and links to Swampy. They fell in love and less than twelve months later baby Horacio was born. But it was not a happy union. Barnaby and Stella had knockout fights that took a heavy toll on young Horacio's mental health and well-being. As an isolated, home-schooled child, he saw no other children and he seldom left the smallholding. At the tender age of six, Horacio was the only witness to the horrific accidental death of a man, which he had never shared with another soul to this day.

'Jaspy, Tobes, get over here,' Horacio says impatiently.

The two boys jump up and scurry across the cave. They slow as they approach Jim.

Flicking his chin towards his captive, Horacio says, 'Pick him up.'

Jasper and Tobias go either side of Jim and hoist him up into a sitting position.

Horacio crouches down to Jim's eye level, places his hands onto his captive's knees and looks sombrely at him. 'If you stay polite I won't hurt you, old boy. Understand?'

Jim nods nervously. The boy's gaze reminds him of looking into the eyes of the small taxidermied deer in his local pub – it makes Jim's stomach twist into a sickly knot.

'What's your name?' asks Horacio.

'Jim.'

'Jim what?'

'Peasnell.'

'Where are you from, Jim?'

'Northampton.'

'Why are you here in the Saltlands?'

'I've been coming here for thirty years. I love it here. It's my second home. I actually have a caravan here.'

'Well isn't that lovely,' says Horacio condescendingly. 'You married?'

'Yes. My wife is probably worried sick. I expect she thinks I've drowned.' His lower lip suddenly begins to quiver.

'Aww, don't cry, Jimbo, we're going to let everyone know you're alive and in secure hands later today.'

'What do you mean?'

'We're going to use you to let all the other scumbag tourists and new Saltlands residents know that none of you are welcome anymore.'

'Why? What have we done? It's a free country.'

Horacio whips out his phone and says, 'It's just gone too far, Jim,' like a patronising teacher. He shows Jim photographs and video footage of littered beaches, traffic jams, a stag party running naked across the sands of Wibli Wobli Bay in broad daylight and a large man defecating on the side of a Saltlands country road. Lastly, he shows Jim a graphic image of a white ferret that looks like it's been pulverised by a steamroller.

'See this ferret, Jim?'

'Yes,' says Jim, squinting to make out the animal. It's barely recognisable. 'I think so.'

'He was my little trooper. I raised him from a kit. His name was Frank. He never hurt anyone.'

Jim swallows stiffly as he watches Horacio's potty eyes moisten.

'Sorry to hear that,' says Jim in a broken whisper.

Horacio growls and puts the phone away. Jim is silently horrified by the young man's instability.

'Frank was slaughtered by the wheels of an English campervan, Jim,' Horacio says, before closing his eyes and continuing his murmuring growl.

Jim blinks three times, unsure how to react. He asks Horacio, 'What are you going to do with me?'

Horacio inhales loudly through flared nostrils, looks up and says, 'Like I said, you play the game, we won't harm you. If you choose to be difficult then I can't assure your safety. Our mission is to rid the Saltlands of tourists, foreign residents and investors, to put it back like it was.'

'Like it was when?' Jim can't resist the question.

Horacio doesn't answer. He just gives Jim a long, malevolent look.

Five minutes later they are on the third take of the hostage video. Jim doesn't have his glasses, so he's finding it difficult to read the cards. They move closer until Jim is able to read the text clearly. Horacio gets the cut he's happy with on the sixth attempt:

'My name is Jim Peasnell and I am a tourist. I have been abducted by the Sons of Blodwyn, liberators of the Saltlands. The Saltlands has been systematically destroyed by people like me – tourists and foreign invaders. We have shamelessly exploited and polluted these lands, so now it is time for us all to leave, to allow the Saltlands to return to its natural state. In order for my life to be spared, all tourists and non-Welsh second homeowners must leave the Saltlands by noon on Sunday, 15th August and never return. If you do not comply, I will be crucified on a wooden cross within twenty-four hours of this deadline, and the Sons of Blodwyn will make a declaration of war against all invaders to these lands.'

Within two hours of the video's 8am social media release, the post has gone viral – over four thousand shares across three platforms.

Despite the 3G and WiFi networks being some

of the weakest in the UK, the video spreads rapidly to all corners of the Saltlands. People are out on the streets by noon and commotion gathers outside many of the coastal cafés and pubs. By teatime, buckets and spades are being packed into cars and the first signs of an exodus are visible. But when the story breaks as a newsflash on ITV Wales News at 6pm, the Saltlands goes into full meltdown, as if a category five hurricane is about to slam into it.

Chapter 8

At 9am the following morning, Keith Beynon, a notorious Saltlands alcoholic and prankster, stumbles into Saltlands police station and notifies Michelle, the receptionist, that he knows the identity of the Sons of Blodwyn.

'How do you know who they are?' asks Michelle, without a modicum of respect. She can't stand the sight of Keith's face.

'Is there a reward for information?'

She rolls her eyes. 'No,' she says firmly.

'Shit. Well, anyway, it's that Fox boy, from the hills. I overheard him discussing with his pals on the sea wall last week about finding a name for their anti-foreigner movement. He was trying to remember Jemima Nicholas's name – you know, that old bird who fought off the French in Fishgu—'

'I know who Jemima Nicholas is, Keith,' says Michelle. 'I went to school.'

'Well, I shouted over to them that her name was Blodwyn, Blodwyn Nicholas. Just for a joke.

I never thought they'd believe me. Christ.'

Michelle studies Keith's face. She can tell he's not lying. 'You honestly think Horacio Fox is behind the kidnapping?'

'A hundred and ten percent.'

'Your eyesight isn't the best, Keith. You *sure* it was him?'

'I can see all the way to the Moon, girl. Without a shadow of doubt, it was Horacio Fox and those two chums of his from away. You know, the ones that are always down in summer, acting like prats around the pubs.'

Michelle nods and says, 'Well, hell's bells. Horacio Fox, a kidnapper. Wow.'

'Why, "wow"? The whole family is doolally.'

Michelle's face relaxes. 'That's rich coming from you.'

Keith grins.

Michelle stares at his thin, tea-coloured teeth and pulls a small face of disgust. 'But there's a bit of a difference in being a little doolally to being a ruthless kidnapper threatening to crucify a tourist, Keith.'

'Is there?' he retorts. 'I don't know, girl. It's a fine line, if you ask me. You'll be surprised. Every one of us is capable of madness.'

Michelle frowns, tilts her head to the side. 'Are we?'

'Aye, we are,' he says in a knowing whisper, before leaning in towards her, saying quietly, 'You ever read *Crime and Punishment*?'

Her eyes widen. 'Dunno,' she shrugs, pausing to think. 'Is that one of them new brochures?' she asks, glancing towards a stand full of shiny new police force publications on the other side of the foyer.

Keith looks across and back at Michelle, mystified. He draws a hip flask from the inside pocket of his donkey jacket and unscrews the metal top. Without taking his eyes off hers he takes a short swig and says, 'Just tell Big Dai what I just told you, alright?'

'Yes boss, right away.'

Her fluffy slippers push down and spring off the carpet, rolling her chair backwards in the direction of Inspector Harries's office, her legs still sticking out straight. 'Dai!' she yells.

'Aye,' Dai shouts back, but he doesn't look up. He's stiffly stabbing an email into his squeaky keyboard with his index fingers.

'Get out here, Dai. You gotta hear this.'

Dai stops typing, peers up over the screen and sees Keith through the slits of the half-drawn blinds. He sighs. 'What does that village idiot want now?'

Dai slots his feet into his cowboy boots, stands

up and struts out into the foyer.

***

Late morning that same day, Angie Pritchard rolls out of bed, stands up straight and stretches her arms high into the air. She pulls on her baggy black pants and a sparkly red sleeveless shirt, walks into the kitchen and puts the kettle on. Sitting around the kitchen table are Scott and Tom.

'Morning,' she says.

'Hey,' Tom mumbles. Scott stays quiet.

'What's up with you, boys?' says Angie, picking up the coffee jar.

'Bad news,' says Tom.

Angie pauses. Her nonchalant eyes harden. 'What?'

They'd spent the previous day on a road trip to Bristol, collecting the final pieces for the casino – a vintage blackjack table and roulette wheel. They didn't listen to the radio all day. They had no idea about the abduction of the tourist.

Tom breaks the news to Angie. She can hardly believe it. '*Crucify*?' she squeals.

Scott picks up the TV remote and puts on the Welsh news. Immediately they're glaring at inconceivable scenes – news teams buzzing around the beaches just a stone's throw from where the three of them are sitting.

Local police and dignitaries are giving interviews, urging calm on the streets of the Saltlands, while drones film the long queues of cars crawling out towards the Hills of Mun, back into Pembrokeshire, and back out east. One English media outlet is peddling a new soundbite along the bottom of the TV screen: *The Saltlands – from the Last Resort to the Sandpit of Hell.*

'Listen to that nonsense,' says Scott, limply raising his hands into the air in protest. 'That's it, guys, the Saltlands is finished. The club is doomed. We're done.'

Neither Tom nor Angie reply. The Flutter Club is almost ready. It's due to open on 21st August, in just twelve days' time.

Tom leaves to give Scott and Angie some space, says he'll go and see what's going on down at Wibli Wobli Bay.

As soon as he leaves, Angie bursts into tears.

Scott looks startled. 'Hey, hey, what's up, babe?' he says, jumping up, wrapping his arms around her.

'My life is just one disaster after the other,' she sobs.

'Don't say that, Ange. This has got nothing to do with you, or me, or anyone else. It's just those nutters that abducted that dentist. It's light years beyond our control.'

'Whatever. Story of my life, Scott. From one cock-up to the next. I'm just a curse, a burden on everyone. Even my own parents don't care I've run away.'

This was true.

Kippers, Angie's brother, had sent a message to Scott just two days ago. The message said that Gary, Angie's father, would not kill Scott if he promised never to return Angie back home ever again. And anyway, her bedroom had already been converted into a karaoke room and bar.

Scott promised, but he couldn't share this news with Angie.

'We'll find a way to sort this all out. We'll get things back on track, Ange. I promise.'

'You just said we're doomed.'

'Nah, didn't mean it. Everyone in the Saltlands is behind us. It'll work itself out once these kidnappers are caught.'

'Behind you and Tom.'

Scott pulls a face. 'What do you mean?'

'People aren't behind *me*. I'm Gary Pritchard's girl.'

'Eh?'

'You know exactly what I mean. People look at me different 'cause of who I am. They treat me different, like I'm a scally.'

'Woah, woah, hold up there, Ange. That's a bit extreme,' he says, knowing exactly what she means.

'The casino is my chance to finally do something. I've never been this excited in my life.' Her eyes sparkle. 'I hated school, failed my exams, 'cause none of it interested me. It wasn't my thing. But the Flutter Club, it's what I want to do. I've never had an opportunity like this.'

'I know,' Scott whispers. 'Me too.'

'Up until now people have been scared of me because of who my dad is. No one has ever really wanted to know me. Half of the Saltlands can't even look me in the eye. But since I met you I've just accepted myself for who I am. I'm not perfect, but I can see I do have things to offer, some skills, some use in life. I'm a good person, Scott.'

'I know, I know, Ange. You don't have to tell me this. I know.'

' She pulls away from Scott and fixes her eyes squarely onto his. 'We can't lose the Flutter Club, Scott, we just can't.'

He nods gravely, easing her back onto him. He runs both hands up and down her back. She drops her head and snuggles into his shoulder. He places his cheekbone on the top of her head. 'I know, Ange. We won't.'

A newsflash appears on the TV. Scott and Angie recoil from their embrace and loom over the flat screen. The suspected abductor of the tourist Jim Peasnell is identified as local Saltlands resident Horacio Fox.

'No way,' Scott whispers.

'That little bastard,' says Angie.

They stand, stunned into silence.

'You know him?' Scott asks, staring at Horacio's mugshot on the TV.

'Know of him. Freak. You?'

'Yep. I know him. He used to be out on the seas a lot with his old man back in the day. Part of the Greenpeace brigade. Always sniffing around, checking what we were up to.'

The newsflash replays Jim Peasnell's hostage video and Scott studies the rock formation in the background. He doesn't recognise it. He pulls the video up on social media and watches it repeatedly. He glimpses a flash of open ocean right at the end as the camera is pulled away from Jim's face. Scott screws his face up and tickles his chin with all the fingers of his left hand. 'That's one of the islands.'

'We have to find him,' Angie says, coldly.

'I know.'

Scott looks at his watch, takes out his phone and rampages through his contacts.

'What are you doing?' she asks.
'Finding us a boat.'

Chapter 9

Mid-afternoon. On their way to the boat, Scott and Angie stop at the police station. It's like Piccadilly Circus – people everywhere. Scott spots Cliffy John sitting quietly on a bench outside, observing all the commotion. He looks relaxed and pleased, even smug. Scott knows the situation plays into Cliffy's hands.

Cliffy sees Scott and blows him a kiss.

Scott rolls his eyes, weaves through the sea of people into the station and attracts the attention of Big Dai by shouting, 'So what you doing about catching Fox then, Dai?'

Big Dai turns to Scott, puts his hands on his hips and sighs. 'Don't you worry, son. We have a patrol boat out scouring the coast as we speak. We'll find him soon.'

'The coast?' Scott says. 'They're on one of the islands! Didn't you see that video?'

'Calm down, boy,' says Dai, clearly irritated. 'We have intelligence that leads us to the northern coastal area. Now if you'll excuse me

I have work to do to bring Jim Peasnell home safe.' Dai pushes past Scott and approaches the waiting journalists.

Scott lingers and listens to Dai speaking to the cluster of reporters. After less than two minutes he pinches Angie's shirt sleeve and pulls her with him as he heads for the door, saying, 'Let's go find fantastic Mr Fox ourselves.'

***

It's approaching sundown, and Jim Peasnell thinks he's holding himself together quite well until Horacio Fox pulls a sword on his two comrades.

'Just go! Get lost, before I cut your heads off, you English bastards,' screams Horacio. He doesn't sound like he's kidding.

Jasper and Toby glare back. They were only trying to persuade Horacio that crucifixion would be almost impossible with the resources at hand in the cave.

They raise their hands submissively and plead with Horacio to let them stay. He refuses and marches them to the blue canoe. They stumble and splash, climb aboard and paddle off erratically. The two boys know it will be pitch-black within the hour. The Saltlands coastline is six miles away, but the sea is calm, so they should make land safely during the night.

'And if you snitch on my location,' Horacio yells out, 'you're both dead.'

The two boys glance back, nodding nervously. Seconds later the canoe disappears around a rocky outcrop and makes a beeline for the twinkling lights of Wibli Wobli Bay.

Horacio turns menacingly to Jim, inhaling a deep lungful of tangy ocean air. Jim is sitting twelve feet away on the damp shingle at the entrance to the cave with his hands still tied up. His face is crusty with salt and dirt. His lip is split from Horacio's thump and a purple swelling hangs below his left eye. Jim is getting so cold he imagines his blood running as thin as copper wire through his veins.

With his sword still firmly in his hand, Horacio locks his sights on Jim Peasnell.

Jim is sure he is going to be killed.

Then, something strange comes over Horacio. He begins to look around suspiciously and to speak in a conspiratorial whisper as he steps closer to Jim.

Jim can't make out what he is saying.

'I'm sorry, I don't understand what you're saying,' Jim says, through dry, shivery lips.

'You can't tell anyone about me, you got that?'

says Horacio, in a louder whisper, his eyes wide and glazed.

Jim is floored by both the whisper on this remote island six miles out to sea and by the less than breaking news that his silence is required. 'Of course,' says Jim, wondering who on Earth he could possibly share his predicament with apart from the curious young seal pup sporadically bobbing around offshore.

'Our secret, OK?'

'Our secret, Horacio.' Nausea churns over in Jim's gut. He burrows into his mind for a way to escape the blond-haired crackpot, but deep down he knows he is at the mercy of Horacio, and prepares himself for the worst.

Instead of advancing on Jim, Horacio walks straight past him into the cave and nonchalantly tosses the sword. It clangs onto the pebbles, emitting a tinny echo around the cave. He picks up Jasper and Toby's blankets, turns around, walks back to Jim and lays them gently across the orthodontist's shoulders. 'I saw you were shivering,' he says.

'Thank you,' says Jim, frowning and bewildered, but happy to feel the immediate warmth of the smothering wool.

Horacio goes silent and looks out over the open sea as if something has caught his attention.

He crunches over the shingle down to the shoreline and pauses to listen. The continued rumble of distant helicopters unnerves him. He knows he's a wanted man with precious little time.

Jim says, 'Why don't you just leave? Take the boat. Leave me here. I'll be rescued and you will have done nothing wrong. I'll say you were good to me.'

'It's too late for that, Jim,' Horacio baulks back quickly over his shoulder.

'Why is it too late?'

'My miserable life is ruined. I won't live much longer, thank God. A sniper will pick me off after I've taken your life, I have no doubt, and I'll be remembered as the freedom fighter who took a stand to liberate the Saltlands.' He pauses, chest inflated. 'Plus, I only have a squirt of fuel left in the tank.'

A peculiar look comes over Jim's face. He shuffles his backside on the shingle and sits up straight. 'Why do you not want to live, Horacio?'

'I have nothing to live for, old boy, that's why,' he says, remaining completely still, looking out over the darkening sea.

'You can't say that. You're only a young man, and you live in the most wonderful place on Earth.'

'You don't know the life I've had.'

'Of course I don't, but "had" is in the past. A young man like you should be looking ahead to the future. Live for the man that you will one day become.'

Horacio turns to face Jim. A twisted, almost embarrassed look reddens his face. 'What?'

'I'm serious, Horacio. You will be someone else in the future – a better, wiser man, and you will look back with pride at this time, a time when you held on through the darkness. Don't mess it all up now, for your sake, please. It's not too late.'

'You're just saying that because you don't want me to kill you. You're sly, Jim, just like all the wretched invaders.'

'But we're not invaders. We're all British. We love this place as much as you do.'

Horacio shakes his head in annoyance and storms back up into the cave. He picks up the sword and begins to slash and slice through the shingle. 'That's not true, and you know it,' he says, his temper rising. 'You saw the photos! Stag parties, littered beaches, defecation on our open roads... even the murder of an innocent ferret,' he yells, stabbing the sword in the air towards Jim's face, now only feet away. 'Do these people love the Saltlands, Jim? Do they?'

Jim recoils, trembling again. 'I can't make

excuses for all that, I deplore it as much as you do, but those idiots are only a small minority.'

'Codswallop. This place will turn into Disneyland in a few short years, unless someone takes action.'

Jim breathes nervously and softens his voice. 'I think you've already made your point by abducting me and releasing that video, Horacio. It's clearly sent people packing back over the Severn Bridge, there's no doubt about that.'

Horacio narrows his eyes, contemplating.

'Listen to the mayhem you've caused! Police sirens all day long, helicopters buzzing all over the skies. It must be chaos back there on the mainland. I think you've achieved what you've set out to achieve.' Jim forces a respectful, fatherly smile, which quickly fades away from his face.

Horacio scratches his forehead with his left thumbnail, weighing his options. 'Nah. Maybe for a short while, but the invaders – they'll be back, unless the fear of terror remains.'

'How can you possibly achieve this all by yourself?' Jim asks, immediately regretting the question.

Horacio's face hardens. 'Quite simple, Jim. I kill you, then disappear *without* taking my own life – just as you recommend.'

Jim tries to swallow, but his mouth is too dry.

He scrambles for words. 'Why would you do that? I'm a good person, and I know you are too. You care deeply about protecting your homeland. If you kill me you will just be a criminal, a murderer. And for what? Once you're caught and locked up the tourists will return. You have your whole life ahead of you, don't throw it all away.'

'Shut up, old man!' Horacio roars and begins slicing the sword through the shingle again, now right around Jim's feet.

Images of his two young grandsons flash across Jim's mind. They're due to arrive later this week. Jim's been looking forward to crabbing with them all year. He is not ready to die. He draws inner strength. 'You will never get away with killing me. There's a huge search party out looking for us. Listen! Those choppers will be here anytime. You should go now, escape while you can, and I assure you I will not speak badly of you. I promise.'

'Sorry, Jim, but I have to make some people around here remember Horacio Fox. They will not laugh and mock when they hear my name anymore, they will respect my legacy, and tell folktales to their grandchildren of my bravery, just as we hear the tales of Blodwyn Nicholas.'

'Bu—'

'Shut up!'

Horacio draws the sword above his head and Jim gently closes his eyes.

Chapter 10

The Saltlands twinkles under the cool ascending Moon, but Cliffy John and Big Dai are feeling the heat. Tucked away in the back room of The Greyhound, the pair are pacing around, staring at their phones, waiting for the pings.

'Why the hell didn't they turn the boat around, Cliff? Christ's sake.'

'I screamed down the phone to Conor, Dai, but the line was all crackly, not sure if he heard. It all happened so quickly. They're in the middle of the sea now, with no signal. They've probably got no clue what's going on.'

Dai blows out air, rolls his eyes.

Cliffy says, 'Those choppers and police boats appeared from nowhere. Why the hell didn't you tell me, Dai? You must have known they were coming.'

'I didn't, until they arrived. The NCA are like the SAS! This was a covert jobby, honest to God.'

'Christ almighty.' Cliffy shakes his head.

Dai says, 'That heroin is heading straight

into the belly of one of the biggest manhunt operations in modern times.'

Cliffy puffs his cheeks and puts his hands over his face.

'Do you realise the ramifications for us if that boat gets rumbled, Cliff?'

'Yes, Dai, I do.'

'Get your phone out and delete every single correspondence with Conor, and between me and you. Text, WhatApp, call history, emails, the whole lot.'

'Aye, good idea.' Cliffy pulls out his phone. 'It's only WhatsApp we use, Dai.'

'Aye, I know. But check everything, I'm sure there's a stray call or message somewhere, there always is.'

'Alright.'

They both stand in silence erasing every shred of potential evidence from their devices and their contact lists from across the Irish Sea.

'Keep trying Conor's phone, yeah,' says Dai, without looking up from his screen. 'He'll get signal soon.'

'I am. Still nothing. Can't we just zip out in the dinghy now? They could be at the cove already.'

'No way, Cliff. There's more surveillance out there now than the skies around Heathrow. Forget it.'

'Might be worth it, Dai? If they get caught and get hold of Conor's phone, we're dead.'

Dai squeezes his eyes tight and rubs his face, saying nothing.

The sound of chopper blades approaches and whizzes again overhead. The search for Horacio Fox and Jim Peasnell has been going full steam all day.

'Christ, it's like Miami Vice out there, Dai. I honestly can't believe the boat hasn't been picked up already.' Cliffy scratches his chin, frowns. 'Maybe it has?'

'No, no. I'd have heard. We've just been scouring the coast today, but at first light we're heading out to the islands. Those are the orders filtering through.

'But then again, with this kind of operation, you never know. They could be searching offshore covertly already. But I don't think so.'

'Can't you do something, Dai? Divert things? Create a smokescreen or something?'

'*Pffff*... fat chance. This isn't your usual Mickey Mouse operation. These are the big boys.'

Dai notices Cliffy's hands trembling as he pumps himself a frothy pint of Double Dragon and downs it in four swallows.

Dai's phone pings. A blue canoe has been pulled out of the water three miles offshore with two men onboard, suspected to be the accomplices of Horacio Fox.

'Looks like we're closing in on the elusive Mr Fox, Cliff. I gotta go.'

'Never mind about him! What are we gonna do about the smack drifting into the Saltlands with our names on?'

'I'm pretty sure we have till daybreak, maybe mid-morning latest, until the boats and choppers go offshore. Just keep trying, you'll get through soon. And when you do, tell Conor to sink the packages, just ditch the gear overboard and get their fishing lines out, OK?'

'But that's almost three hundred grand's worth, Dai!'

Dai's eyes almost pop out of their sockets. 'What? Jesus. I can't believe I'm hearing this, Cliff. Have you lost your marbles, man? We'd go down for decades if they find the gear and Conor's phone. Just get it sorted, *get it ditched*, 'cause the cavalry will be on top of them before noon, I can guarantee it.'

'And from now till dawn, what's happening? They still searching?'

'No. All the search craft are on their way in now, till daybreak, I'm pretty sure.'

Cliffy ponders for a moment, then says, 'Hells bells, we're pushing it, Dai. I don't know if my ticker can take any more.'

'What? *You* were the one who wanted to keep going! Just a little bit longer, you said. It's never enough for you, Cliff, is it? Until it's too bloody late.'

'Piss off, Dai,' Cliffy snarls back, pumping another glass full of ale.

'Just a stupid, greedy, reckless bastard,' Dai mutters as he exits through the kitchen door.

Cliffy hears. 'Up yours, Dai,' he yells back as the door slams shut. 'You don't call me stupid in my own pub,' he mumbles, draining the second pint. He puts down the empty glass and belches loudly.

Cliffy turns and reaches for a dusty holdall that is scrunched up behind the bar and loads it quickly with a giant Maglite torch and a waterproof rain jacket he finds hanging on the pegs. As he steps to leave he leans across and rips four bags of pork scratchings off the cardboard wall-mounted holder in a mini fit of rage, slams them into the bag and lumbers towards the kitchen door.

***

Puffin Island, 2am – the most southerly of the small offshore archipelago. Like all the islands, there are no sandy beaches, just steep granite cliffs plunging into the cool, blue Atlantic. Narrow coves and coarse storm beaches frequent the exposed south-westerly side of the islands, where pirates and smugglers had passed treasures and contraband for centuries in the dead of night.

Scott and Angie idle the boat reluctantly around the island. Discretion is impossible with a motor and a searchlight. Scott knows they're sitting ducks, but his twelve bore shotgun is loaded and he's ready for the fight of his life.

As they cross to Shearwater, the next island, Scott receives a message from Tom. There are rumours that Horacio's two accomplices have been captured out in the bay. The rumours also suggest that Horacio is now alone with his captive on one of the islands, but there is no confirmation of which of the nine islands it is.

Scott widens his tired eyes. 'We're gonna find this son of a bitch before dawn, if it's the last thing I ever do.'

Angie huddles up to him at the wheel and drapes her arm across his shoulders.

Scott goes quiet, lost in his thoughts, remembering the old days fishing these very islands, the memories still crisp. The cold, damp days in squeaky rubber waders, heaving pots of crab under the dismal, crushing fog.

The gnawing, cawing seagulls lined up on the gunwale, the driving rain, almost willing them to give up. But then there were *those* days, the one in thirty, when the rising sun would beam through the wispy clouds and illuminate the fibres of the coastline and the blueness of the ocean to create a natural landscape like no other, dissipating the darker memories in a heartbeat. But all this time was work. Relentless work. The only constant in Scott's young life that bore him fruits; fruits now set to rot by the actions of the deranged. He steels himself and idles the boat onwards through the dark night.

A fog bank settles over the boat just as they reach the southern tip of Shearwater Island. Angie feels a chill in seconds and shudders.

Scott says, 'Bollocks. Can't see a thing now.'

'Well, Fox can't see us either.'

'True, true. We'll be fine,' he says calmly. 'I know every nook and cranny of these islands.'

The searchlight bores through the heavy fog and the hull scrapes lightly along the seabed as it moves through the water, as close as Scott can push it. But Shearwater is clear, no sign of life, just gently lapping waves on its empty shores.

Angie looks up through a break in the fog and spots a band of stars, tangled and thick. 'I think it's clearing, Scott. Maybe we'd better scoot to the next island quickly.'

'Aye aye, Captain,' he says, without a hint of humour. He's entranced, still scanning the Shearwater rockfaces like a trained cyborg.

Gannet Island, the third island, and Scott is aware this could be the one. It's littered with coves, some uniquely on the sheltered eastern side, which Horacio will be aware of, Scott is sure.

Scott picks up his twelve bore and checks both barrels again. He locks the gun gently and flicks off the safety switch.

Angie is startled. Her heart leaps into her throat. 'Why are you doing that? You think he's here?'

'We're getting closer, Ange, there's no doubt of that.'

As they approach the northern tip, Scott says, 'Ange, come here, you take the wheel.'

'What?' I can't steer a boat.'

'It's easy. You've seen what I'm doing. Just keep it going like that. You can stay out a bit deeper. They could be on this next stretch, there's a couple of sheltered coves here, so keep your wits about you.'

'OK,' she says, more confidently, taking the wheel.

'And if I shout "go", just open the throttle up and zip away from the island as fast as you can, yeah?'

'Really?'

'Aye. You'll be fine.' He winks and kisses her on the forehead.

Angie settles behind the wheel and steers the boat around the contour of the island like an attentive learner. Scott steps up to the bow and draws the shotgun to his eye line, the searchlight dangling off the two small fingers of the hand nursing the barrel. The beam shines squarely on the rock face just metres away.

The first cove comes slowly into view. Scott has his finger on the trigger and feels an electric surge of adrenaline through his body.

Nothing.

They idle forward towards the next outcrop on the southern tip of the cove. Scott momentarily drops the gun from his sights and rolls his head quickly around, twisting his anxiety away. The bow approaches the outcrop and Scott again raises the gun and searchlight. The cove is illuminated by the beam, and there, sitting in the middle of the small shingle bay, is Horacio Fox, with Jim Peasnell between his legs, a sword blade pulled firmly against the orthodontist's pale, skinny neck.

Chapter 11

Cliffy approaches the back door, devouring the last mouthful of an egg roll, the dusty holdall in his left hand. He pauses, swallows and wets his lips, running through his mental checklist. *Check*.

After threading the spinner to the line, Cliffy places the rod carefully into the boat. He starts the engine, the rasping noise tearing through the quiet night.

He feels queasy as the boat idles out of the inlet, a diffused feeling of anxiety, paranoia and determination. His face looks ghoulish in the green glow of the pilot light. He chooses not to look back, just forward into the wide open blackness.

He's only going fishing. That's all. Nothing peculiar about that. He's not been paying attention to all the commotion these past days. He's got enough on his plate. His pubs are failing. Bloody Covid. He's stressed out. Fancies a bit of night fishing. Peace and quiet, out in the elements.

His anxiety eases as the inflatable craft cuts between the heads and out towards the islands. He opens up the throttle. The bow rises up and pokes at the crescent Moon hanging low in the sky.

***

'Do you remember me, Horacio?' asks Scott, half-yelling from the boat down onto the beach.

'Of course. Why are you here?' Horacio shouts back, wiggling himself upright in the shingle.

Scott instructs Angie to cut the engine. She does so immediately and the cove falls silent.

The sounds of the sea fill the damp air.

'We've come to ask you to stop what you are doing. Please let that man go. It's affecting a lot of people, in a bad way, and most of us are already in a desperate situation.'

'That's not my problem. I'm just trying to protect the Saltlands from all the invaders, like this scumbag. Haven't you seen what they're doing to our home?'

Horacio tugs the long blade a little deeper into Jim Peasnell's neck.

Jim's body goes taught. He whimpers.

'I hear you, Horacio. The tourists are pissing a lot of us off as well, but many of us need the opportunities they can bring, especially after Covid. We're supposed to be a community here in the Saltlands. Surely you know that. And feel part of it. We can manage these changes together, and use them to our advantage.'

'I don't belong to any community. Never have.'

'That's not true. You've grown up here. You're one of us, man.'

'That's bollocks, and you know it.'

'What do you mean?'

'You know what I mean. I've never been accepted.' Horacio pauses, sucking in air to steady his rising heartbeat. 'People hate me, or they think I'm a joke.'

'No, they—'

'Shut up! They do!' Horacio screams back.

Jim yelps and Horacio retracts the knife a fraction of an inch.

Scott and Angie stay silent on the boat.

Horacio rubs his espadrilles back and forth on the shingle and they start to sink into the damp stones. He looks up. 'The land is my community, the land of the Saltlands, not you people.'

'Yes, I know. And the sea was *my* community. You know I've spent most of my life alone, out in the ocean. But this place – this land, this sea, breeds and attracts some good people, Horacio. Kind people who love nature, who want to preserve it, like you and me.'

'Kind? Ha! Rubbish,' scoffs Horacio. 'I always thought that my life growing up alone in the hills was a nightmare, but when I began to try and make friends everyone in the Saltlands just blanked me, and made me *feel* alone, which was actually much worse.'

Scott sighs. He looks across at Angie and prompts her with his dancing eyebrows.

Angie steps out onto the deck and says, 'I understand you, Horacio,' in a husky feline voice that's soothing and sweet. 'I know there's nothing worse than being with people who don't understand you.'

'Who are you?'

'I'm Angie. I'm from the Saltlands too. Atlantic Drive.'

'And?'

'Well, like you, I've felt rejected and alone since the day I was born because of who my dad is.'

'Who's your dad?'

'Gary Pritchard.'

'I've heard of him. He's that psycho.'

Scott and Jim Peasnell raise their eyebrows at the same time.

'Well, to me he's just my dad. But yeah, he's a bit rough around the edges, and he's a lazy, useless bastard. But worse than that, he always made me believe that I was never good enough. He's always made sure I'm insecure, if you know what I mean. I've been at rock bottom for most of my life. Never been able to accept myself. I've always felt alone.'

'That's dads for you,' Horacio quips.

'At least you both have fathers,' says Scott. 'Mine died before I was even born.'

Horacio frowns. 'What do you mean?'

'He died, in an accident. He was a fisherman.'

Angie edges nervously out towards the bow and says, 'Erm, be honest, Scott. He committed suicide. And it ruined people's lives.' She turns to face Horacio. 'And if you don't stop what you're doing with that man, Horacio, you will end up ruining lives too.'

Scott's face reddens. 'He didn't jump!' he screams across at Angie.

Angie looks stunned.

'What the hell do you know anyway?' he scowls at her. 'You weren't even born then. *Everyone* says he fell off the cliff.'

Angie drops her head.

Horacio blinks furiously and the back of his head begins to tingle. 'Can't be,' he whispers to himself. 'When were you born?' he shouts up to Scott.

'What?'

'Just tell me – when were you born? Which year, and which month?'

'1996. April. Why?'

Horacio lets go of the sword, which drops into Jim Peasnell's lap. Jim doesn't move.

Horacio stumbles backwards on the shingle, loses his footing and falls. He stands up again, but his legs feel heavy, like he's wading in quicksand. 'Why are you here? Why are you messing with my head?' he crows, falling limply onto his knees.

Scott and Angie look bewildered.

'Are you OK, Horacio?' asks Angie.

'He fell,' Horacio says.

Scott says, 'What?'

'Your father, he fell. He fell off the cliff. I saw it. I saw it!'

Scott looks confused. 'I don't understand what you're saying, Horacio.'

'The morning of the oil spill – I was there, in a boat, with my father and my uncle. I was young, but I remember it like it was yesterday. We went to see the grounded oil tanker. The sea was black, and the smell... and I saw a man up on the cliff. It was really early morning. Daybreak. He was doing something, bending down, trying to reach for something. And he slipped. He slipped! He didn't jump.'

The sound of small, lapping waves fills the silence.

Scott looks down at Horacio with piercing eyes. 'Do you swear it, Horacio?'

'I swear to you.'

'You saw my father fall off the cliff? In February 1996?'

'Yes. Yes. Yes.'

'Why should I believe you?'

'Believe what you like. It's true.'

'Are you sure?' asks Angie.

'Sure? *Sure*?' Horacio says, now annoyed. 'Jesus, it's been playing over in my head every single day since it happened. It was an accident. And it was awful. I'm sorry.'

Scott puffs his cheeks, squats down, and places the gun gently on the deck of the boat in front of him. Some moments later he says, 'I'm sorry you had to witness it, Horacio.'

'What's done is done. It was a long time ago.'

'Well, for what it's worth – thank you,' Scott says sincerely as he sits down and puts his head in his hands. He fights to hold back his tears.

Horacio lies back on the shale and vents out some air through his lips. He looks up at the thick band of stars splattered across the big sky. His eyes widen and he grins. 'Glad to be of service, Scott.'

Angie shimmies over to Scott, bends down and puts her arm across his shoulders. She pulls him towards her and looks down onto the beach and sees the Moon catching on Jim Peasnell's face. He looks tarnished and empty. He hasn't moved. The sword still lies across his lap. He lifts his head and makes eye contact with her.

'Are you alright, Jim?'

He nods gently, clears his throat and says, 'I just want to go home.'

***

Cliffy is quietly jamming the two packages into the dry bag when Conor starts the engines of his boat.

Cliffy cuts him a sharp look and shouts, 'What the hell are you doing?'

'Going home, Cliffy lad.'

'I said wait for me to buzz back! I only need half an hour. Please, Conor.' But Cliffy's voice is drowned out by the motors.

'So long, cowboy,' Conor shouts with a grin. Cliffy winces. The boat banks to the side, gouging a deep gash of white water into the black sea. Within seconds it disappears around the headland, making a beeline across St George's

Channel in the direction of Wexford.

Cliffy stands helpless, enveloped in engine fumes that remind him of bubbling asphalt in summer. He's alone with two kilos of black tar heroin with a street value of over a quarter of a million pounds.

He pauses for a second to think, then throws the sealed bag over the side of the boat. The bag's tether shoots through his hand as the bag sinks. He leans over the port side and follows the tether all the way to its source – a clip, submerged under the hull.

He starts the engine and opens the throttle. His hands are cold and damp on the wheel. The glistening lights on the distant shores of the estuary flurry like a searing mirage as he bounces towards it.

He knocks off the throttle at the estuary's mouth, gliding the boat in slowly. His almost unshakeable self-assurance returns and a smug look spreads over his face.

A blast of light from a pontoon on the northern side of the shoreline dazzles Cliffy. Primal panic sets in. He opens up the throttle and swings the boat almost a hundred and eighty degrees in a heartbeat. The engines scream as they tear back out into the open ocean.

The bright light stays illuminated on

the pontoon and silhouettes of men move
purposefully around it. Voices begin to grow, and
shout.

Chapter 12

Horacio stabs his feet down through the creamy salt water, searching for the seabed. He makes contact. He wades out of the water and up onto the beach, panting, charged with adrenaline. He darts behind a hunk of nearby rock and peers out to try and get a glimpse of the new arrival in the speedboat.

Five minutes previously, Scott and Angie were startled by the sound of the boat approaching from the direction of the small bay just to the south of them.

In response, Scott ignited his engine, swivelled the boat around until the bow was pointed out to sea and picked up his shotgun. Angie tucked in behind him and held on to his wiry hips.

Horacio took this distraction as an opportunity to escape the beach, to flee from his captive – Jim – and from Scott and Angie. But the only way out was around the headland to the south, in the direction of the approaching speedboat, to the neighbouring bay, which Horacio knew had trails leading up the cliff face onto the top of the island where there were places to hide. The opposite way, going north from the cove, was just sheer, flat-faced cliffs plunging into the sea – no place to hide.

Cliffy points the speedboat squarely into the shallows and onto the beach lying to the south of where Scott and Angie are. The hull crunches through the shingle, sending a shiver up Horacio's spine.

Cliffy cuts the engine and the cove falls silent, but the sound of Scott's boat, idling out of sight in the neighbouring bay, soon reaches Cliffy's ears. His alarm levels skyrocket. He shuffles along the port side, reaches over the side and begins to reel in the tether like a bloated madman.

Another hypnotic sound starts to radiate through the long night, growing in intensity with each passing second. The blade chop of a helicopter. Not one, but two, zipping across from the mainland, just a single search light beaming down onto the still ocean from each of the giant machines.

Cliffy stands up straight on the boat and listens. His body goes rigid. He holds the dry bag filled with heroin tightly in both hands.

Horacio observes Cliffy from around eighty feet away. He doesn't recognise him, but he can tell he's not come to the island in search of him – Cliffy is clearly lost in his own dire predicament.

Horacio shivers, looking on curiously as Cliffy frantically empties the contents of the bag under the soft glow of the Moon. Horacio assumes the two small bales in Cliffy's hands are Class A drugs. What else at this time of night?

Five hundred yards away, Scott and Angie realise Horacio has disappeared from the beach. Scott leaps off the boat with his gun and his light. He scans the cove, the cave and the shoreline, but there is no sign of Horacio.

Scott knows he must have swum to the southerly bay, towards the commotion. There was no other option.

Angie pulls Jim up onto the boat. He's weak, and his smudgy eyes are sunk deep into his bony head.

Scott returns to the deck and the three of them look up into the sky as the choppers approach, but they can't see them from their position inside the small bay. Scott steps up to the helm and propels the boat southwards, closer to Cliffy, to Horacio and to the approaching helicopters.

In the last moment before the helicopters are upon him, Cliffy stuffs the two packages back into the dry bag along with a large adjustable metal spanner. He zips and folds up the bag and slices the tether with a knife, freeing the bag from the rope. With great effort, he throws the bag out to sea. It lands with a weak splash and sinks about thirty yards from the shoreline just as the helicopters come into view.

Cliffy sits down, quickly unhooks the lure from the lower eye of his fishing rod and holds it in his hands, studying it, as the searchlights illuminate him in the middle of the lonesome bay. It's 2.48am.

The maelstrom of wind and noise from the helicopter blades unsteadies Cliffy as he tries to stand up, a surprised and bewildered look on his face. He raises both hands into the air. His straggly grey hair blows wildly around his square, balding head.

A rope drops down from the forward helicopter and four black silhouettes descend, like a scene from an old Vietnam war movie, Cliffy thinks. The troopers draw firearms when they hit the shingle.

They instruct Cliffy to get off the boat.

At that moment, Scott's boat curls around the headland and into view, surprising the four armed men. Two of the troopers move their rifles to point towards Scott, Angie and Jim. The air quivers. Scott glides the boat calmly to the shore, pulling up next to Cliffy's. Angie puts her hands up and screams, 'We've got Jim Peasnell!' and points madly towards Jim, but the turmoil of noise and wind drowns her words.

A helicopter searchlight swivels and beams brightly towards the three of them. Jim cowers, throwing his arm across his face, burying his eyes in his elbow joint. They all hang there, suspended in time, waiting for something to happen. It does.

A Border Force boat zips into the bay with its own beaming lights, carrying four more armed troopers in dark combat clothing. The boat is small – a rigid hull inflatable from the large cutter ship out at sea, manned with more armed personnel. The cavalry have arrived. The lead trooper on the beach signals to the helicopter pilots to leave. They simultaneously bank the machines off in opposite directions, dip the noses and charge off in unison back towards the coastline, leaving a welcome silence behind them.

Horacio is quietly clawing his way up the cliff face. He has picked up a long piece of anchor chain off the beach. It's coiled around his shoulders and neck, rusted and heavy, making his progress along the rock face difficult. Soon he's perched over the sea, shuffling towards the headland, likely hoping to tuck away out of sight once he gets to the point, just thirty yards or so ahead.

The lead trooper yells, 'Where is Fox?'

'This is Jim Peasnell!' Angie screams, holding Jim up by his elbow.

'Are you alright, Jim?' shouts the trooper.

Jim is fully illuminated and squinting. He raises both thumbs up into the air and shouts, 'Horacio is here! He's here, around this beach somewhere.'

Scott twists up his face, half-hoping Horacio will be able to escape. He looks across at Angie. He can sense she feels the same.

'Look for him, for Christ's sake!' Jim yells. 'Before he gets away.'

The head trooper baulks instructions into a microphone on his chest and his squad deploys briskly around the pitch black bay. Head torches slash around like lightsabers. Two troopers enter the water and move like beavers towards the jagged granite outcrops.

'What the hell are *you* doing here?' Scott yells across to Cliffy.

'Fishing.'

'Fishing?' Scott squeals. 'At this time? You?' He begins to laugh.

Cliffy's face stiffens. 'OK then, if the truth be told, I was actually coming after Fox myself. I had a hunch he'd be here after seeing his little video, so I thought I'd come and try and do my bit for my community.'

Scott's mouth hangs open. 'Really? "Your bit for the community?" Ha! Honestly, I've never heard such crap in all my life,' he says, shaking his head. 'Councillor Cliffy John, actually getting off his arse and doing something for the Saltlands community... to the point of risking his *own* life in the middle of the night to save a poor, unsuspecting *English* tourist? Pull the other one.'

Yelling comes from the northern flank of the cove. Horacio has been spotted. He's stranded, high and dry, up near the point, on a wall of jagged rock as light beams begin to illuminate him. He's a sitting duck. Assault rifles hone in on his head and back.

Horacio tries to look over his shoulder, but the thick chain restricts him. He reaches down and grabs the dangling end and loops it around his neck, which is already laden with three coils of the rusted metal links.

'What the hell is he doing?' whispers Scott, and with that, Horacio releases both hands from the cliff face and grabs onto the chain around his neck. He wobbles, then plummets like a tombstone through the air. His feet hit the water with force and he sinks quickly, disappearing without a trace.

Scott screams, 'Horacio!' and dives off the side of his boat. He crawls quickly through the water, fully clothed, and reaches the spot where Horacio disappeared just seconds later. He sucks in a lungful of air and dives down into the water. His ears pop as he plunges deeper. His eyes are wide open, burning, as he searches madly in the heavy blur.

Horacio sits cross-legged on the sand bottom, his hands still gripped to the chain around his neck. He's blowing bubbles from his lips, emptying his lungs, longing to exit this world. He sees a shadow flash across him. He tries to fight it off, but he can't. He feels the chain unravelling from around his neck, unravelling his destiny. His body releases from the seabed, and he begins to float, he tries to fight it, but the shadow is now under him, driving him upwards.

Horacio breaks the surface and gasps air into his lungs. Scott surfaces beside him and ferries Horacio into the shallow water just metres away. They collapse onto the shale like two drowned rats, hyperventilating.

Horacio's blurred vision starts to clear as he looks around him. He blinks and it takes him a moment to catch on. A small crowd has gathered on the shoreline in a semi-circle around where he and Scott are lying. Six of the troopers have assault rifles pointing at his skull. He doesn't care. He sees Angie and Jim, before sweeping his eyes to the solitary man furthest away along the beach, almost out of the frame. It's that man, the man from the speedboat. Horacio lifts his right arm and points towards Cliffy John. 'That man. That man over there,' Horacio says, still panting. 'I think I need to tell you... to tell you something about him.'

Epilogue

Cliffy John was found guilty of playing a leading role in the trafficking of two kilograms of Black Tar heroin into the United Kingdom, and for money laundering the financial gains of these illicit activities through his chain of Saltlands pubs over a five-year period. He was sentenced to fourteen years in prison.

Cliffy represented himself in court, assuming, naively, Big Dai would have pulled the necessary strings to get him off with a light penalty. Cliffy pleaded not guilty to all charges, claiming he had found the dry bag of heroin that night on the beach during a night fishing trip and thrown it out to sea in a panic when he heard the approaching helicopters. The fine shreds of tether still attached to the bag told a different story.

Passing sentence, the judge noted Cliffy had wholeheartedly abused his position of trust and responsibility as a local councillor, and that, despite the well-publicised deaths of young people from Black Tar heroin, Cliffy continued to traffic the toxic substance, calling his actions nothing short of 'evil'.

'Big' Dai Harries was not implicated. Cliffy had nothing on him, and Dai had hedged his bets by whispering into Cliffy's ear the morning he was brought into the police station that he would do his best to get him off. Cliffy believed this great lie. Dai stepped immediately away from the case and swore to himself he would remain clean until the end of his days.

The case brought against Horacio Fox was compelling, involving charges of drugging and abduction of a random and innocent victim. Horacio, filled with remorse, pleaded guilty to all charges. His family's barrister pushed the judge for leniency in sentencing on grounds of diminished responsibility. Several mental health assessments confirmed that Horacio was unstable at the time of the crimes, and statements from Scott, Angie and even Jim Peasnell painted a positive picture of a young man with strong moral principles that should be shown some degree of clemency.

Horacio was sentenced to three years and six months by the Crown Court judge. The sentence was classified as an imprisonment by hospital order, whereby Horacio would be detained securely in a hospital rather than a prison, to provide him with ongoing mental health rehabilitation.

The Saltlands bounced back. Within days of Horacio's capture, the tourists began to make the midsummer pilgrimage out west again over the Severn bridge. Covid-19 was still lurking, but it was under control, and life was back to some kind of normality. International borders had reopened, but domestic British tourism didn't slow down and continued to thrive for the first time in decades.

Jim Peasnell's abduction had captured people's imaginations and made international headlines as far away as Australia and New Zealand. This gave the Saltlands a new found fame and notoriety. Dreamers and social media influencers streamed down the M4, through Pembrokeshire and over the Hills of Mun to the Saltlands National Park. They came to follow Horacio Fox's footsteps through this windswept outpost of desolate beaches and marshland, and out to the now infamous Gannet Island – the setting of the rescue, which was purportedly already being scripted for the big screen.

Wibli Wobli Bay became like the Waikiki of west Wales – surfers and water sports enthusiasts living the sun-kissed dream. They slept in beaten-up campervans, sat around campfires, played guitars into the wee hours, creating a new scene, connecting with each other in those long, flickering shadows – talking, laughing, singing together as if it was altogether something completely new.

The coast path was alive with hikers from north to south, the towns bustled and small business throughout the Saltlands was booming. Something was happening, things were changing, and they were changing very fast. The abduction had brought everyone together, given a sense of perspective of what was important, what they all had, and how lucky they all were to call the Saltlands their home. The future was looking good, for the first time in decades.

Horacio's actions and words had an impact. The Saltlands Council cited the motives behind Jim Peasnell's kidnapping as a contributing factor to their decision to ban all single-use plastic items and all polystyrene containers from the Park by the end of the year. In the same meeting there was also a verbal commitment for the Saltlands to achieve carbon neutrality within five years.

***

17.58pm, Saturday, 28 August 2021

Angie is making tiny adjustments to the chairs and stools around the bar, making the seats all perfectly lined up and symmetrical. She listens to the growing commotion outside the front doors and feels a wave of nervous energy wash over her.

Scott walks past her and steps down onto the old dancefloor carrying a container full of gambling chips. He is wearing a shirt for the first time since he went to see the bank manager, or to a funeral. He can't remember which.

Tom is counting out the till floats, nodding his head gently to the subtle electronic beats that will form the soundtrack to the slick and glamorous Flutter Club. They've made it just as they imagined it – a place for locals to come and enjoy good food and drink, to have a dance, and maybe a little flutter on some of the vintage gambling machines and card tables. Scott calls it their 'good times emporium'. The phrase sticks.

'OK, Scott, dim the lights!' Tom shouts across the big hall.

Scott reaches over to the switchboard and flicks three switches. It darkens and the room is transformed. Pools of intimate light illuminate the playing tables and the bar looks electric.

At 18.02 chanting comes from outside, calling for them to open the doors. The trio do their final checks. The staff are primed and ready to go. Excited glances ping around in the last moment of calm before the storm.

Scott, Angie and Tom walk together, hand in hand, to the front doors. They push them wide open, and a roar of excitement fills the Saltlands sky.

Acknowledgements

Thank you to Sam Groves, Moira Jenkins, Matthew Lowe, Ayumi Martin, Vicky Morris, Mark Murphy, Julie Owen and Annabelle Wilson for reading and for conversations. Particular thanks to my mentor, Laurence King. Most of all, to Jess and the boys.

Quick Reads

Quick Reads offer a series of short, engaging books which appeal to all tastes and reading abilities for the price of £1 each, encouraging less confident readers to pick up a book. These titles are aimed at adults who find reading a struggle or who've lost the habit of reading, and are also perfect for readers who are short of time. The initiative is coordinated in Wales by the Books Council of Wales and supported by the Welsh Government.